THE CONFESSIONS OF A

BACKSLIDER

BY

HENRY CLAY MORRISON

First Fruits Press
Wilmore, Kentucky
c2013

ISBN: 9781621711278 (Print), 9781621711285 (Digital)

The Confessions of a Backslider by Henry Clay Morrison
First Fruits Press, © 2013
Pentecostal Publishing Company, circa 1930

Digital version at
http://place.asburyseminary.edu/firstfruitsheritagematerial/72/

For all other uses, contact:

First Fruits Press
B.L. Fisher Library
Asbury Theological Seminary
204 N. Lexington Ave.
Wilmore, KY 40390
http://place.asburyseminary.edu/firstfruits

Cover design by Haley Hill

asburyseminary.edu
800.2ASBURY
204 North Lexington Avenue
Wilmore, Kentucky 40390

The Confessions of A Backslider.

By

Henry Clay Morrison,

Author of

"World Tour of Evangelism;" "Thoughts For The Thoughtful;" "Life Sketches and Sermons;" "The Two Lawyers;" "Baptism With The Holy Ghost;" "The Second Coming;" "The Pearl of Greatest Price." Etc.

PENTECOSTAL PUBLISHING COMPANY, PUBLISHERS
LOUISVILLE KY

CONTENTS:

———

THE CONFESSIONS OF A BACKSLIDER.

CHAPTER I.

EARLY REMINISCENCES.

Few people living have an adequate conception of the powers of the human mind to grasp and retain the things that pass through it in a lifetime. I have had ample opportunity to experience the marvelous powers of memory. A man's mind is like a great storehouse or depot in some seaport in which a thousand things may be stowed away. They are perhaps forgotten, time passes, but by and by some clerk will take a waybill and search from room to room, garret to cellar and drag out dusty bales, boxes, and packages, that had not been thought of for months, but there they are with the proper stamp and address upon them. So it is with a man's mind. It is stored with a multitude of things that, for the time, he has forgotten, but when occasion arises and he rummages through the garret and cellar of his memory the past events rise up with familiar faces and look him in the eye.

I cannot say that I have been a hard student. The fact is I never did give myself up to industrious study of a language, a branch of science, or difficult and hard problems. I didn't have the industry in me that calls for that kind of work,

but I was a great reader, fond of histories, magazines, novels, stories of travel, and all that sort
of thing, and from my boyhood I delighted in
reading, and early in life formed the habit of reading late into the night. When reading an interesting novel, I have sometimes read all night long
and it was quite a common thing for me to read
until one and two o'clock and then lay abed late
the next day to the inconvenience of other people.
In this way, I contracted the habit of wakefulness
and could not sleep until late at night, rarely going
to bed even when I had nothing to read, before
one o'clock. When I was locked up in the institution from which I write these chapters (and I
may as well in the outset confess that I write from
a prisoner's cell) I found myself at great disad-
vantage because of these irregular habits. The
light is turned out on us here promptly at nine
o'clock and then I must lie in total darkness and
think, while the clock strikes ten, eleven, twelve,
one, and sometimes two, before I can find relief in
sleep. Could I have had a light in my cell, and
books to read, I never would have realized the re-
tentive powers of my memory. But, without a
light, lying in the darkness, I have learned to en-
tertain myself with reflections on the past, and I
have been surprised to find that all of my past life
is written indelibly on the pages of memory. It
seems that I have really forgotten nothing. I have
been able to go back to my early childhood and to

follow myself through life to this sad, dismal place, in a remarkably minute and accurate way. The acts of my life, the places where I have acted, and the very dates, have been burned into my brain.

It has occurred to me that there are some things connected with my sad career that may be communicated to others to their advantage, so I come to you with some of the fragments of the story of my misspent life. I should regret to appear to blame others for my misdeeds and for the calamities which have come upon me. Nevertheless, as my identity is completely concealed and as what I shall say cannot bring any sorrow or hurt to those of whom I shall speak, I shall not hesitate to try to describe, to some extent, the influences that went into the building of my character which made me unfit, and unable to battle against the temptations before which I have fallen.

My father was a good man. He was not a man of college education, but had been to the common schools, and was a man of natural ability, read many good books, kept up somewhat with the political and general news of the times, and was quite a reader of religious books and the church periodicals. He was a diligent man in business and accumulated quite a comfortable living. He was a positive man, almost to sternness, a man of just principles and a tender, true heart.

My mother was my father's second wife. He

had one son by a former marriage who was a boy
ten years older than myself, my brother John, my
ideal and delight. Poor, dear John! He was
deeply fond of me, played with and cared for me
in my childhood and loved me faithfully to the
last. It is some comfort to me that my father
and John both went away in peace to heaven before I brought disgrace upon the family.

My mother was a graduate of a woman's college.
A place where they gave more attention to exact
grammar, careful pronunciation and correct spell-
ing than they did to the higher things that belong
to the soul. Not that I have anything to say
against thoroughness in education, but my dear
mother was much more careful of my mental
training along these lines than she was in the de-
velopment of my moral character. She was much
more anxious that I should learn how to speak
grammatically than she was that I should learn
how to make an honest living in the sweat of my
brow. Poor woman! She always seemed to feel
that I was too precious to do good, honest, hard
work with my hands; one of many deluded moth-
ers, with whose unfortunate sons I am now associating in a place where we are forced to do the
work that we were, unconsciously, taught to avoid
when we might have done it in honor and happiness.

My mother had taught school a few years before
her marriage to my father and had developed quite

a spirit of controlling other people. She never was able to get over this and it was always a question who was the head of our house, and not infrequently we children heard discussions at the table and about the fireside between our parents, which were most unfortunate in their effect upon us and our general family government. I remember well it was the occasion of great disappointment and sorrow to my boyish heart when I was made to realize that my parents did not have the affection and love for each other that is necessary to a genuinely peaceful and happy home.

My parents were church members. They were also religious, but they failed to reach that state of piety that would deeply impress their children with the importance of seeking early the one thing needful. I was a wilful child, selfish, hard to control, and while my father was inclined to be severe with me, my mother was quite inclined to be indulgent. Perhaps both of them went to extremes and they rarely, if ever, agreed with each other with regard to what I should do, what I should wear, what books I should study, what places I should visit, with whom I should associate, or how I should be corrected and dealt with for my many disobediences and misdeeds. In the end, my mother became my champion and protector, and gradually my father sadly and unwisely, yielded to the situation and gave me up. I can remember so clearly when I began to realize that my mother and myself were getting the victory over him and coming to rule the house as we chose, and I began to feel that I could largely do as I pleased without any fear of punishment. The thoughtful reader will agree with me that these circumstances were most unfortunate for my child life.

From my very early childhood I attended Sabbath school and was carefully instructed in the great doctrines of Christianity, and believed them very firmly and many times had a strong conviction in my heart because of my disobedience and sinful acts. There is no memory that stands out more vividly before me than the revival meeting in which I was converted. I was just turning into my fifteenth year. There were evangelistic services held in the Methodist Church of which my parents were members. It was a great time of awakening, and many of my schoolmates and best friends were saved, myself among the rest. I need not go into details, but I had a great struggle of soul. There was a strong bent to evil in me, but finally I surrendered and after many tears and much earnest praying, was soundly converted. I can never forget the sweet peace and joy that came into my heart. For quite a number of weeks I ran well, kept company with earnest young Christians and enjoyed the various services of the church, but my early training had not put into me the kind of character that makes stalwart Christians. A child who has not obeyed his parents will find it difficult to live in obedience to the law of his God. While I soon lost the first glow of love which came into my heart at the time of my conversion, I kept a tender conscience and my faith in God, the inspiration of the Scriptures, the deity of Christ, and the personality of the Holy Ghost was clear and unshaken. If I could only have gotten into a Christian school I might have become established in my spiritual life and have made a happy and useful man, but my going away to college proved my undoing.

CHAPTER II.

OFF FOR COLLEGE.

My parents took a deep interest in my education. They had ample means to give me a thorough college training and however they may have disagreed about other matters concerning me, they were united in their purpose to give me good school advantages.

I do not care to name the college to which I was sent. The president was a large man of striking appearance, varied learning, and wide experience in the world. He was genial and warmhearted and the students loved him devotedly. While he was a member of an orthodox church, in his religious convictions he was quite in harmony with the modern higher criticism, and I think a sort of Unitarian without any firmly fixed faith in anything only that he was not in sympathy with any orthodox or evangelical preaching, and frequently made light of what he called "sudden conversions." In his chapel addresses he used to say that he did not like the expression, "getting religion;" that a man got religion like he got an education; that every man was the architect of his own character, that good deeds were like so many bricks laid into a wall of good character. That we must not be looking for some outside influence, or power, to save us or make us happy, but that we must live right, be honest, tell the truth, and despise little and mean things. I think the man worshiped at the shrine of his own works. He had a very attractive and eloquent way of presenting his thoughts. He rarely, if ever, mentioned Christ or the atonement made by him, and I am confident I never heard him mention the Holy Spirit. He talked much of manhood, of self-reliance, of independence, of becoming good by doing good, and all that sort of thing.

My teacher in natural science was quite a bright and fascinating young man, enthusiastic in his advocacy of the teachings of Darwin. It was his delight, in a covert way, to ridicule preachers, to point out what he claimed were contradictions in the Bible and boast of his determination to be free from the dominion of the priesthood and to do his own thinking. I well remember that he took the entire hour of one of our recitations to lecture the class on the fact that the orthodox Christian faith had become obsolete, and many of us were quite surprised at the large number of university and college presidents he cited as having turned away from the Scriptures and being in harmony with the views advanced by himself.

Under these influences I neglected the Bible, prayer and church, and finally I gave up my faith, and came almost to hate the Bible, and joined with other boys in ridiculing the old faith. I well remember how, while passing through this stage of my experience, I sometimes awoke in the night with a great ache in my heart and a solemn fear would creep over me that I was being led astray, but our professor taught us that these fears were mere superstitions and were common to all heathen people. "There is nothing to fear," he would say, with a great show of assurance.

The pastor of the church we attended was quite in harmony with the spirit that characterized the college. He preached much on historical, scientific, and literary subjects. He was quite an orator and large numbers of students attended his church, especially at night when he gave us sermons or lectures on Shakespeare, Browning, Longfellow, and other distinguished literary men. It would have been difficult for any student of my age to have maintained his simple faith in Christ as a Savior from sin under the pressure which was brought to bear against us. I am confident that a number of our professors were delighted when they saw the boys drifting away from their religious moorings. They said it was an evidence of growth in a fellow to find him doubting the legends and superstitions which had been taught him by people who had not had the advantages of modern, scientific education.

Gradually all of the anxiety and fear connected with the change which was coming over me, passed away and I exulted in a sense of liberty and felt quite free to think and do as I pleased, and soon learned to laugh at any protest of my own conscience. It startles me as I reflect on the moral condition of that institution of learning. Boys who came there with good religious experiences and a clearly-defined faith in the great doctrines of Christianity, were soon robbed of their belief, their spiritual life was destroyed, their consciences benumbed, and directly they were playing cards, drinking whiskey, swearing profanely, and falling into those vices which hardened their hearts and polluted their bodies. Not unfrequently students were sent away from the institution because of having contracted loathsome diseases from which it seemed impossible to recover them. As I reflect over the wrong that was done me and many of those bright young fellows, I can but feel that our teachers will be held responsible at the judgment bar for the manner in which they trifled with our faith.

As all interest in spiritual life died within me, a great love for college sports took possession of me and I wasted my time, neglected my books, and deceived my parents in order to indulge my abnormal love for sports. The money which my father sent to me to defray my legitimate expenses, I wasted in following my college baseball team from place to place, having him afterward to suffer embarrassment and inconvenience by having my bills sent to him for settlement.

I was a poor student, lost interest in my books, and after two years left the college, which I first attended, and went farther east to a large and popular institution where I found less of faith, more of immorality, and stronger temptation to indulge my abnormal desire for the excitement of the various college sports, and for games of chance, in which I was frequently indulging.

After four years in the two colleges mentioned, I wasted two more years in a university where I was fully confirmed in the unbelief and skepticism which had taken root in me in the colleges of which I have spoken. I am amazed as I look back at the bitter prejudices which seemed to possess both teachers and students in these institutions against the Bible, against the doctrine of the virgin birth of Jesus Christ, against the sinfulness of sin and the beauty of holiness. I do not believe ministers and religious people of this country have any true conception of the condition of unbelief and immorality that exists in many of our great seats of learning. Whatever may be said of the education to be obtained in them, of the opportunities for scientific study and research which they afford, I assure my readers that there is, in many of these great schools, a condition which tends to brutalize men, to give them a low appreciation of every sacred thing, God, the church, womanhood, the home, the civil law, and everything that ennobles life and makes good character permanent and beautiful. In many of our schools there is a subtle drift toward anarchy; disregard of divine

law and human law, a tendency toward the belief that every man should be a law unto himself.
A diabolical feeling that there is no sacred Sabbath, that it is stupid to regard one day as any
better than any other day, that there is no such
thing as sin, that there is no harm in adultery, in
taking advantage in business transactions; that
after all life itself is not the sacred thing that the
Bible would make you believe it to be; that we are
to be governed by the great law of "the survival of
the fittest," and that every fellow is to get the most
out of life for himself that he can, largely regardless of his fellow beings. It is this spirit that has
led to revolts and strikes in some student bodies
that has at times seemed to threaten the existence
of some universities.

Of course no professor says these things point
blank in lecturing in classes, but as I have intima-
ted there is a strong under current drifting in this
direction. As already stated, I was at no time a
hard student, but picked up quite a smattering of
knowledge of history, literature, geography, and
the sciences. I was proficient in nothing. In
these schools I enjoyed many social advantages
which gave me a certain polish that enabled me
to pass for a gentleman and has paved my way
to the sins and crimes which have brought me to
the cell from which I write these letters, with the
hope that some one, reading them, may take warning and avoid the snares into which my feet have
become entangled.

CHAPTER III.

BEGINS A FAST LIFE.

When I finally returned home from college, without graduation, but somewhat disgusted with myself and yet without the shame and reproach that I ought to have felt because of my repeated failures, my father was very anxious for me to go into business with him, but, knowing his serious views of life and intending to be free from the restraints which I felt he would place upon me, I accepted a position as bookkeeper in a large livery and sale stable in the city. Here, you may be sure, I came in contact with a class of men who were of no moral advantage to me. I had become passionately fond of baseball and spent much of my time reading the sporting newspapers and indulging in loud conversation and heated disputes over this, that, and the other champion—losing not a little of my salary betting on my idols.

The first thing I stole was the time that belonged to my employer. When I ought to have been busy with my bookkeeping, I was at a baseball park, race track, or pool room. Frequently he spoke to me about my negligence and I made promises and many good resolutions but did not have in me the power to keep them. The wasting of one's time, which has been paid for by one's employer, is the beginning of dishonesty that will deaden the conscience and lead by and by, at least in many instances, to the appropriation of money.

I spent almost two years on my first job and then secured employment as a commercial traveler. I succeeded very well in this business and got a good salary, but wasted my money in fine clothing and high living. Occasionally I visited my father who was growing old rapidly. He was what is called a "hen-pecked" man. He had resigned himself to the situation and had become a deeply pious man and spent much of his time reading his Bible and, I have no doubt, lived a life of true devotion. When I would visit him, he showed the tenderest concern for me and frequently tried to talk to me about my wild ways. I could see that he was full of anxiety and fear for my future, and while I treated him with courtesy, I felt perfectly safe and independent of all his counsel and warnings; thus the time went by, my heart growing harder and I drifting further and further from the path of righteousness.

My brother John became a Christian when but a boy and always looked on the serious side of life. He was not a melancholy man, but a sober man. He was a fine student and graduated from college with honors. While in school he commenced preaching and directly after his graduation entered actively upon his life work of preaching the gospel. John followed me with many letters, good books, and prayers. I neglected his letters, read but few of the books he sent me, and felt a sort of pity for him that he should be so dull as to imagine his prayers were of any account to me.

After about a year on the road, I learned to play cards successfully. I played at first for small sums of money to make the games exciting, and finally, as I became more expert, I bet to win money and was sometimes quite flush never winning large sums but frequently up into three figures and perhaps three or four times reached four figures. I thought quite well of myself and was beginning to believe that I was quite an expert with brilliant possibilities ahead of me at games of chance; but frequently I was so badly beaten at cards and horse races that betting, for a time, lost its influence over me, and I gave myself more diligently to my business and, for a few months, saved up my money with careful economy, only to risk it again and lose; while I did not give up my employment, I spent many a night at cards.

There is no more exciting and dissipating life than that of gambling. Games of chance stir the blood, excite the mind, affect the nervous system, break down the morals, assassinate the conscience, and degrade a man as few things practiced among men. Constantly on the road, spending almost every night in some pool room or gambling den or theater, I became passionately fond of excitement and gave almost no time to the companionship of religious friends or the reading of books of any kind except the most exciting works of fiction.

All the time I had a great faith in, and a great love for my brother John and would frequently visit him; his influence calmed me. I delighted to take long walks with him and talk over our early life and the happy days we had spent together. He was pastor of a large church in one of our northern cities, which had been builded for middle-class people in a thickly settled residential part of the city. Most of his people were poor, at least in moderate circumstances. In his church there was a widow who kept a small millinery establishment and did quite a prosperous little business. Her daughter, a tall, graceful, beautiful girl, sang in John's choir. This widow and daughter took the greatest possible interest in all the meetings held at the church, both of a religious and social character. On visiting the place, I was strongly impressed that they had designs on John and gave him a word of warning. He spoke very earnestly of their sincerity and devotion as Christians and their deep devotion to the church, but felt that I was mistaken in their feeling any selfish interest in their pastor and I saw in the course of the conversation on the subject, that John was quite fond of the young lady and was not surprised, some months later, when I received an invitation to attend the marriage of John to the pretty daughter of the milliner. Somehow, I had learned that the girl was the discarded sweetheart of a medical student and felt that she was not the girl for John to marry, but attended their wedding and hoped in my heart that she would make the wife that so true a man deserved.

Directly after his marriage John was moved to another city and to quite a prominent church which paid him a very respectable salary. At once the mother of his wife closed up her establishment, went out of business, and went to live with John and his wife, and I noticed how readily they assumed considerable superiority, put on all manner of high-toned airs and sought the association of the most wealthy and cultured people, not only of John's congregation, but of the wealthy class living in the neighborhood of his church.

I shall not forget how angry I became on visiting John sometime after he had moved to this new field of labor when, at the table, his mother-in-law absorbed most of the conversation with a dissertation on the kind of husband a man ought to be; how he ought to provide for his wife, how he should treat her, and how he should shield her from hardship and how patient he should be with her in her various nervous states; in fact an eloquent lecture on the duties of a husband, with many remarks on what a woman's needs were, how impossible it was for a pastor's wife to meet her social and church obligations without certain servants and various equipments. She talked as if John were receiving a salary of four or five thousand per year instead of fifteen hundred. John bowed his head in meekness, was deeply in love with his wife, and had learned that when his mother-in-law proposed to give a lecture it was best to remain silent. I spoke to him about it afterward. He admitted that the situation was unfortunate but could see no way out of it and was quite disposed to go forward making the best of the circumstances.

John's wife soon purchased a fine bred, fox terrier puppy, on which she lavished much of her time and affection. A little later on, she was quite inclined to become a fashionable invalid and spent no little time at the telephone calling up the drug store and asking for advice from a handsome, young, infidel doctor, whom she had selected as her family physician and whom, I learned afterward, had been an intimate friend of hers while attending medical college in the town where her mother kept the millinery store. From some friends I learned that this young doctor was quite a reprobate, and suggested to John that it would be wise to secure an older and more experienced man for his family physician. He said it would suit him to have some one else, but that this man was an old friend of his wife's and she preferred him to all others.

Having had quite a little experience with the world and its wicked people, I had a very uncomfortable feeling over the drift of things in my brother's home and although far from what I should be, I loved John devotedly, and was jealous for his happiness and usefulness.

The doctor suggested that my sister-in-law attend a certain watering place through the summer. Her mother went with her, John paying the bills for both of them. I made it convenient to drop into the place about ten days after they went up and was not surprised to find that the young physician was spending his summer vacation at the same watering place and he and my invalid sister-in-law were having rather a gay time together. I left the place without any of them knowing that I had been there or had observed their movements, but with a spirit of vengeance burning in me, making up my mind to say nothing to John but that if I was fully convinced of infidelity I would take the matter into my own hands.

CHAPTER IV.

SEEKS REVENGE.

In the fall of the year I made my headquarters in the city where my brother was preaching, securing rooms in a hotel only a few blocks from the parsonage. My sister-in-law and her mother seemed quite displeased that I should be so near a neighbor, but I made it a point to see but little of them and conceal from them my knowledge of their distaste for me. Meanwhile I took a devoted friend into my confidence, and, without the young doctor suspecting it, kept a close eye on his actions and found plenty of material to confirm the fears I had for sometime harbored.

Up to this time, wicked as I had been, I had never taken a human life or felt any desire to do so. As I have already said, I had become a gambler. I had stolen my employer's time and in representing my goods and settling up accounts with the firm for which I labored and their various customers with whom I dealt, I had not been strictly honest and yet I by no means looked upon myself as a thief but my heart was hard and wicked and bitter hatred was rising in me and I could feel the spirit of murder taking possession of me. I had secured a pistol which I carried constantly and, frequently passing the young doctor's office, I felt like stepping in and shooting him down at his desk.

If I could have induced my brother to leave his wife, I would have cheerfully given every dollar I had to have taken him to any part of the country or over the seas or anywhere to get him entirely away from her and her influence and the disgrace that I felt, sooner or later, she would bring upon him. But knowing his love for her, I never breathed a hint of my suspicions to him. Frequently I would be out of the city for weeks and sometimes months at a time and my mind would become somewhat relieved on the subject that agitated and enraged me, but on my return my confidential friend would tell me of things that had occurred during my absence and would throw me into a frenzy of anger and yet neither of us were positive that I would be justified in shooting the wretched man on the basis of the unwritten law.

The next summer John's wife again went away to the watering place, the young physician went up and spent his summer vacation and I drifted along in his wake and looked with venomous eye on his devoted attentions to the beautiful, silly woman, who was breaking my innocent brother's heart. John was so devotedly in love that he was quite blinded to the faults of his wife and yet her treatment of him had become such that he had been forced to conclude that she had no real affection for him.

I shall not go into the details of what followed,

but suffice it to say that directly after my sister-in-law's return from the summer resort, my brother went away from home to spend a week at a religious convention. My confidential friend sent me a telegram to come at once to the city. He met me and we talked together and arrangements were made. That evening, which I remember with a shudder in my poor soul, my friend and myself went to the parsonage, it being near midnight. I crept quietly to a back porch where a back door led to an alley way. At a given moment, my friend rang the door bell violently; all was quiet. He rang again and then beat with his fists upon the door. I heard a noise in the house and directly the young physician, with his coat on his arm and his shoes in his hand glided from the back door on to the porch. I had an electric flashlight in my hand and threw the glare of it in his face. I shall never forget his startled look as he recognized me. No word was spoken; it all occurred in an instant. The electric light was in my left hand, the forty-four in my right, and there was a tremendous crash. The muzzle was within a few feet of the poor fellow's left breast, and he sank to the floor without a word.

I ran rapidly through the alley and down a back street for three blocks, came out quietly into the street with a cigarette in my mouth, entered the hotel at the side door and went up a back stairway, threw off my clothing and leaped into bed and assumed to be sound asleep when some one beat on my door and said there was a telephone call for me to come instantly to the parsonage, my brother's residence. I dressed hastily, ran to the telephone, and called up to know if anyone was sick. My brother's mother-in-law said: "For mercy sake come quickly and bring a physician with you if you can find one convenient." I left word with the night clerk to send the hotel doctor around at once, and ran to the house. I found my sister-in-law fainting with hysterics, her mother wild with excitement. They said an awful murder had been committed on the back porch. They supposed that possibly two burglars had met there and fought with each other, that they heard a pistol shot and the mother-in-law looking out of the window could see the dead man in his shirt sleeves without his shoes on. She supposed he must have been undertaking to rob the house and had been shot dead.

I called for a lantern and going out with the doctor, who had by this time arrived, turned the unfortunate man over and the mother-in-law, who had followed me, screamed out, "Why it is Dr. George Prater!" The coroner was summoned, the undertaker was called, and the next morning a little after daylight the dead body was taken away. I telephoned my brother to come home at once and I shall never forget the look on his sad, white face when he came. His wife was in a hysterical condition, he did all he could to solace her but she refused to be comforted. A few days later she was sent to a sanitarium and my brother, being granted leave of absence from his church, went away to visit our father.

The newspapers were full of accounts of the tragedy, the reporters indulging in all sorts of guesswork and imaginations. No one seemed to suspect me of being in any way connected with the unfortunate affair. The young doctor seemed to have no near relatives in the city and those best acquainted with him, knowing his character, said that his untimely death was the logical sequence of the course he had followed, let his blood be upon his own head, and so there was no special effort put forth to ascertain the cause of his death, or who was the perpetrator of the deed.

Being a little afraid to hasten away lest I should be suspected, I remained in the city for several weeks and flattered myself that I succeeded in wearing an air of perfect innocence. Afterward I went about my business as usual, traveling here, there and yonder, and carrying with me a load much heavier than I had anticipated as I had thought over the matter. As I lay awake many nights reflecting over the matter, I thought of many better ways out of the trouble than the one I had chosen. I condemned myself for my action upon the ground that the woman was not worth the price I had paid in seeking vengeance for my brother. I deeply regretted that I had not left the family to their fate trusting my brother in the merciful hands of the Christ he loved instead of madly determining to blot out the life of a fellow-being.

The thought of this tragedy has haunted me through the years. Sometimes I have almost succeeded in convincing myself that I did right, but then my better judgment, like a rising tide, would sweep away the frail barriers that I had tried to build, and I would again have to admit my unwisdom and the great wickedness of my action. I grew restless and found that I was incapable of attending to business and would hurry from town to town and city to city, hardly taking time to show my samples or to take orders from the merchants who desired to purchase goods from the firm I represented.

I had resigned my position and was making arrangements to join Gomez in Cuba and help the patriots in their struggles against the Spaniards, when war was declared against Spain. I at once joined a volunteer regiment and was thoroughly glad that my regiment was ordered to the front, hoping that in the excitement of battle and becoming familiar with death, would have the effect of quieting my anxieties and relieving my mind of the distress which had fastened upon me because of the sad tragedy that now hung as a black cloud over my life.

The excitement attending our landing in a new country, the strange and interesting surroundings, the effect of marching, the thrill of battle, the benumbing influences of walking about among dead men, did very much to occupy my mind and, for the time, I found not a little relief from the gaunt specter that haunted me. Sometimes I felt like it would be best to so expose myself that I would be killed, at other times I was inclined to rush headlong into all manner of sin and try, if possible, to so harden my heart that I would be without feeling, and then again, I would wonder if it was possible for me to repent and find that pardon I had once enjoyed, but in these better moments the skeptical teachings that I had imbibed from my unbelieving teachers in college would rise up and chill my soul, and I would hope that after all we were all only well developed apes, hardly responsible for what we did. And thus I was tossed about twixt hopes and fears. Although I laughed loud, and recklessly, I was a very unhappy man.

CHAPTER V.

ARMY EXPERIENCES.

There were a great many young college and university men in the volunteer army during the Spanish-American war. No one looked for a long war or much serious fighting, and we all believed in our superiority over the Spanish soldiers as fighters, and many of us young men looked upon the war as a sort of outing or picnic and went in for the excitement of it and a jolly, good time generally. The fighting did not amount to so much, but there were some distressingly hot moments before it was over, and a number of fine young fellows were cut down by bullets and a great many more, in fact some thousands of the boys, were swept by disease into untimely graves.

Strange to say in those days and nights about the camp fire, while I was trying hard to persuade myself that I had certainly ascended from apes, and that it mattered but little if one ape should kill another, I found myself quite inclined to talk on religious subjects. My distressed state of mind drove me to seek to confirm myself in unbelief. If I could only have found some one who could have proven to me, beyond a doubt, that the Bible was a concoction of stories and fables gotten up by uninspired and designing men it would have lifted a load off of my guilty soul.

I was not much surprised, and somewhat comforted, to find most of our college and university men, especially those from the East and Northeast, were unbelievers in the Scriptures. I met with quite a number who, like myself, had once been Christians but had been robbed of their faith in the Scriptures, in the schools they had attended, and, like myself along with the giving up of their faith, had given up their morals also, and had become miserably wicked men. Skeptical college professors seem to forget that the old faith which they regard as musty superstition, has a powerful moral effect upon men's lives; that it lifts up high standards of honesty, sobriety, and virtue, and these in the way of promised rewards and punishments, offer most powerful incentives toward a right course of conduct, and true manly living. There is that in the nature and surroundings of a young man, that draws him very strongly toward an improper and dangerous course of conduct. An unquestioning faith in the Bible and the future life, revealed in its pages and what it says of the final fearful outcome of sinful conduct, places a powerful restraint upon a man. It gives him both hopes and fears to check and brace him to resist temptation and to develop strong and pure character.

The modern destructive critic in the college or pulpit, destroys this wholesome faith in the Bible, takes off the restraints, unbridles the appetites, cuts loose the letch of the passions and sends

young men into rampant wickedness. Of course,
that is not their purpose, nevertheless it is almost
certainly the result of the course they pursue,
many of them are doubtless acquainted with the
facts, and yet seem perfectly willing to take the
risk involved in the propagation of their free and
easy notions about the inspiration and authority
of the word of God.

The soldier in the United States army finds very
little to restrain himself from sin, or to help himself to a life of purity and right living. A large
per cent of the army officers are materialistic in
their views. They too have the taint of unbelief
that is so common today in many of our schools,
and among a large per cent of the public men
of the country. Comparatively few army officers,
whatever their views may be with reference to the
Scriptures or the religious life here and hereafter, wield an influence that has any moral effect
upon their soldiers. The chaplains themselves
seem to be for the most part, political chaplains.
That is, they were men who had a pull. They were
not appointed to the chaplaincy because of any
especial fitness for the position, but because they
had friends who were able to secure for them
the position and they went along for the money,
the recreation, and the novelty of it instead of to
watch over and protect the boys from the ruin of
army life.

It is wonderful how the social vultures will

gather about an army camp. The very worst of
men and women come flocking in there from all
quarters and settle down around the soldier boys
to live off of them. Saloons and brothels, gambling dens and dives, will spring up like mush-
rooms at any place where soldiers are stationed for
even a few weeks. In the Cuban campaign, the
people swarmed like flies about our camps and
the sin and degradation were something fearful.

Just after the war closed, and while we were
still in camp in Cuba, I received a letter from
my father telling me of the death of my poor
brother John. It turned out that John had been
suffering from diabetes, and while the doctors felt
that the tragedy which had occurred at his house
had broken him down and perhaps helped to hurry
his trouble, nevertheless the die had been cast for
the poor fellow, and it would have been impossible, under the most favorable circumstances,
for him to have lived but a short time. This
aroused all of my compunctions of conscience. I
could see now if I had let the matter entirely
alone, John would soon have gone away in peace to
heaven and been saved beyond those so unworthy
of him, to live and sin as they saw fit, and I would
have had no blood on my hands, no guilt on my
conscience.

John's death seemed to be the breaking of the
one last link that held me on somewhat to hope
for better things, and I seemed to fall away deeper

into unbelief and indifference than before. I
plunged into excess, frequently drank to drunken-
ness, gambled away what money I could get my
hands on and rushed into sin, not only to gratify
my carnal inclinations, but with the deliberate
purpose of so hardening my heart that my wicked
enjoyments might not be disturbed by the cries
of my conscience. Wicked as I was, I do not suppose that I was any worse than a very large per
cent of my associates. I do not think that the
average minister of the gospel has any real conception of the amount of sin that is going on
around about him, of the number of fearfully
hard men one will meet with in a day who live as
if there were no Bible, no God, no judgment, and
no hereafter. So far as any outward observation
is concerned, that is the way a very large per cent
of us lived in the army. And, as to that matter,
sad to say, in many of the great colleges and universities.

When the Cuban war closed, I came home for a
time, found my father in rapidly declining health,
and deeply concerned for me. While he looked
upon me with great solicitude and I could easily
imagine his thoughts, he was careful of his words
and the dear man did not dare to exhort, entreat,
and warn me as I am sure his heart ached to do.
As for my mother, I have chosen not to discuss her
in these articles. I might say however that she
was quite a proper woman, attended her church,

had very rigid notions with reference to table etiquette and other little things that she magnified into matters of great importance, devoted herself largely to literature and gave some attention to philanthropic movements most of which concerned people over the seas and far away. I doubt not she had real love for me, and there was yet lingering in me enough of the human to have a very tender regard for my mother; in fact, too much for me to say more of her in these articles.

I remained at home but a little while; found myself restless and without any desire at all for employment or care for setting myself up in business, or looking ahead to the accumulation of property, or what people called success. The army suited me better than anything else, so I re-enlisted with the regulars and went to the Philippine Islands, where I lived as the animal, I had been taught in the university to believe myself to be —an army brute of sin. I found, in the regular army, more men than you would think who had had some advantages in the world, but, like myself, had made poor use of them and were now seeking to bury themselves alive. We had but little fear of death and the lives of others were not sacred to us, so the camp, the raid, the skirmish, and the excitement of man hunting, suited us about as well as anything in which we could have been engaged to kill our time and throw our miserable lives away.

During my time of service in the army I found several soldiers, who, like myself, were carrying a burden of blood; had been connected with killings, one way and another on account of women, sweethearts, wife, or sister. I think in every case they had lived to regret the folly of their rash deed, and like myself, they were seeking to drown the voice of a guilty conscience in the noise and excitement of army life.

Men may ridicule the old Bible all they choose, but those who trample upon its commandments will, in the end, kindle within themselves a fire of torment they cannot put out. Sometimes they may flatter themselves that they have about extinguished it, but it will break out and blaze up afresh, consuming all their happiness and all their hopes.

CHAPTER VI.

A DELIGHTFUL ACQUAINTANCE.

When my three years' term in the army expired, I started for the United States, but stopped off in Hongkong, ran up to Canton, and knocked about considerably in southern China. I fell into bad company as was my habit, and my little savings, received from Uncle Sam at the close of my term of service, were soon swept away in drinking and gambling. I worked my way on a steamer to Shanghai expecting to seek employment, earn some money and return to the United States. But it is easy when one is well on the way down the hill to go from bad to worse and at Shanghai I drifted into fearful depths of degradation. I failed to find employment in Shanghai that would give me anything like good remuneration, simply picking up a job here and there, became discouraged, and spent most of what I earned for bad whiskey, stopping at once of the cheapest lodging houses I could find and lying around the wharf to help load a ship, or discharge a cargo, or pick up any odd job that came in my way.

Frequently, when recovering from one of my drunken sprees, I was strongly tempted to commit suicide, often trying hard to persuade myself that the teachings of my college professors, who sneered at the Bible and made so little of human life and the hereafter, were correct, but the memory of my experience of my early boyhood clung to me and although I sometimes stood upon the brink, I feared to take the leap into the dark.

It was when I had reached a very deep depth of degradation and hopelessness that an incident occurred which was really a turning point in my life. I was working on a small steamer that ran down from Shanghai to the mouth of the river to meet the incoming ships. As the channel of the river is not deep enough to permit the large ships to come up to the city, they anchor near the mouth of the river and small steamers run down to bring up the passengers. One day we were bringing up quite a large company of people. I was, at the time, fireman on the boat, and being quite warm had come up out of the boiler room to catch a breath of fresh air. I was covered with perspiration and the dust and grime from the cool I had been shoveling, and certainly in my bloated and red-eyed condition I presented anything but an attractive appearance. As I leaned on the rail of the boat, a group of elegantly dressed and unusually handsome ladies sat on the lower deck conversing with each other. It was so delightful to hear the English language spoken by Americans, that I turned about and looked at the party, almost unconsciously gazed at them, when one of the women, a beautiful creature with golden hair, fair face, and blue eyes, looked up to me and asked the distance from the mouth of the river to Shanghai.

When I answered her, "About twelve miles," she smiled beautifully and said, "Excuse me, but you are an American," to which I answered that I was. Upon this she asked me with reference to my native state and on my telling her that I was from a certain state, "Why," she said, "that is my state," and upon further inquiry it turned out that I was quite well acquainted with the city in which she had been born and raised and in which she now had her home. She came and stood with me by the rail of the boat and we conversed for several minutes. Under the spell of her charming influence I forgot my soiled and disgusting appearance and also forgot my duties until the stern voice of the engineer aroused me and called me back to my coal heaving.

During our conversation I learned that this young woman was going out to visit her brother, an American gentleman who was connected with a large business firm in Shanghai. While I had no acquaintance with her brother, I knew of his business firm, something of his reputation as a substantial man of affairs and knew him when I saw him on the street. Fortunately he did not know anything of me.

After I had fired my engine and just as our boat was pulling into the landing at Shanghai, I again went on deck and was surprised and delighted that the fair young woman, with whom I had been talking, as she came out with some hand baggage, looked up and nodded me a kind good-bye, and catching a beautiful rosebud which was pinned at her breast and handing it to me she said, "Take that to remember a friend from your old state over the ocean." I do not think that I ever had a possession that I prized so dearly as that little flower. Poor prisoner that I am tonight, with my little effects in a box here at my feet, treasured away in a piece of oiled paper and shut up in a little case made out of cedar wood with my own hands, is that precious little rosebud. Somehow through the drifting years it has been a sort of link that has bound me on to hope and again and again, when it seemed that I was ready to despair, the rosebud has reminded me of the smiling and beautiful face that thrilled me with some of the noblest desires that ever came into my depraved heart.

1 heard the young lady remark to some one of her group of companions that she expected to remain in Shanghai for at least a year, and that night on the ragged soiled bed in the old shack in which I lived, I lay awake and dreamed of the past and the future. I thought of the golden opportunities which I had thrown away, of the cultured people with whom I had once been associated and the miserable creatures among whom I now lived. I was able to see myself by contrast. I could but compare the beautiful young woman with the fair face, golden hair and beaming eyes

with my own bloated, sin-burdened and begrimed
self. There seemed to be a great gulf fixed between us so wide and deep that there was no hope
that I would ever be able to cross it, but a strange
change came to me that night.

I determined to give up the use of strong drink
and tobacco, to work hard, to save my earnings,
and to strive to at least be a decent human being.
I will not undertake to tell the reader of the tremendous conflicts I had with the appetite for
strong drink, but I won the fight. I was receiving fairly good wages on the little steamboat and
saved my money with greatest care. Within two
weeks' time that little rosebud had lifted me out of
the old shanty into a fairly respectable boarding
house and by the end of a month I was decently
dressed and in my leisure moments avoided the
vile portions of the city of Shanghai and walked
the decent streets and was pleased and comforted
when anyone spoke to me in my own language.

I went to the American Consul and told him
something of my story, of course keeping back the
worst part, but informed him that I had served
in the army and was anxious for a more remunera-
tive and respectable position than the one I now
held. Through his influence, I was able to secure
a clerkship in a freight office on one of the large
wharfs at quite a good salary and a few weeks
thereafter had a little bank account, was stopping
at a nice boarding house and wearing the first

tailor-made suit I had had on since I first joined the army.

The reader may be sure I had not forgotten the beautiful woman who gave me the rosebud. By following her brother from his business house, I located his place of residence and also found out where he, with his wife and sister, attended church. I had not been inside of a church in many years, but I fully realized that unbelief and the wickedness which had come along with it had been my undoing, and, influenced no doubt more by the woman of whom I had spoken, than by any desire to become a Christian man, I commenced attending church. The services were rather formal; the preacher was not a good speaker nor did he seem to feel the power of the truths he was proposing to proclaim. I suppose I was a poor listener and very incompetent to judge of the good qualities of a sermon; at all event, I did not seem to derive much benefit from the preaching. But it was a change and a change for the better and the novelty of it entertained and somewhat refreshed me. The singing sounded very sweet and took me back to the days of my boyhood, reminded me of my dear brother, John, and his warm heart and earnest Christianity.

While I had given up faith in the Bible, or at least tried to do so, I could not give up my faith in John, and while I had striven hard to doubt my own immortality, I could not for a moment help believing that John was somewhere in a conscious state of existence, and that he was in a state of peace and happiness.

During my time in the army and the dissipation which followed, I had sadly neglected reading, but I now secured some good books and when not engaged at my work put in much of my time reading and in six months from the time I had come so unexpectedly into the possession of the beautiful little rose, I was a very much changed man. I was no Christian, but I was sober. My heart was not changed, but there had awakened desires and longings in me which were certainly drawing me in the right direction. My health was fully restored. I stood six feet tall in my stocking feet and was a robust, well proportioned man with strength above the average.

As the time went by, I was promoted, my salary increased and in some business matters I was brought in contact and became acquainted with the brother of the young lady I had met on the steamboat. He in turn introduced me to his wife and sister at the church and in due time I was invited to visit their home where a delightful acquaintance sprang up between myself and Miss Rosalind Fawnsworth. This was the name of the woman who by one little act of kindness had started me on the road to better things. Of course, I said nothing of our previous meeting and it would have been impossible for anyone to have recognized me as the poor bum to whom she gave the little flower that had done so much for me.

I frequently walked home with her from church and occasionally took her out for a drive, was introduced by her to a group of intelligent and interesting people. It seemed that a new era had dawned upon me and I sometimes felt as if genuine happiness was a possibility, and I should have been happy, but for the sad secret I carried hidden in my heart. A man who takes the life of his fellow-man shoulders a fearful burden to carry through life. Only those who have had the experience that has haunted *me* can have a real conception of the unrest that attends the man who has taken away the life of his fellow. The specter leans with him over his books at the desk, walks with him on the street, sits with him at the table and is hanging on his bedside when he goes to his restless pillow, startles him from his slumber, and grins with a cruel familiarity in his face when he arises from his broken rest to meet another day of remorse. I would that those who may read these lines may fix a deep resolve within their hearts to be saved from the burden I had so foolishly taken upon my shoulders. In spite of it, however, there was hope rising up in me for better things.

It is useless for me to tell the reader that I was passionately in love. The object of my affection was in every sense worthy. She was of good fam-

ily, educated and accomplished. She had a high
moral sense, she was a Christian with an unclouded and restful faith. She was tender-hearted and
compassionate, and was full of cheerfulness; there
seemed to be no unkind thought or impulse about
her. She was one of those women in whom a
man could confide absolutely. Like all true women, she was genuinely affectionate, and as the
days went by, although a modest and reserved woman, she gave frequently cause for me to believe
that she had some feeling for me other than mere
friendship which so readily springs up between
people from the United States who meet even casually in the far away oriental countries.

CHAPTER VII.

DEEPENING FRIENDSHIP.

I now began to feel an interest in life I had never known before, and devoted myself to business with great earnestness.

Notwithstanding I had failed in the proper appreciation of my school advantages, nevertheless I passed easily as an educated man and had picked up much information in college, university, army and foreign travel, and such reading as had come to me, all of which enabled me to be quite useful to my employers who evidently thought well of me and advanced me in my work until my salary was sufficient to keep me comfortably and put by a neat little sum of savings.

The change which had come to me was quite remarkable. Next to the religion of Jesus Christ, there is nothing that will so powerfully influence a man as an ardent love for a good woman. As the time went by I received encouraging indications that my attentions and devotion to Miss Fawnsworth were genuinely appreciated, and I will not delay the reader with details of a story which is thoroughly interesting to me, of how I courted her and won the pledge of her love.

For a while my past was at times almost blotted out of my memory, and I was a happy man. My way was clear, save for a small cloud upon the horizon, which now and then swept across my sky.

No man can be genuinely happy who does not believe the Bible and rest his faith in Christ. He may have pleasures, hopes, and many blessings, but he is an unanchored man, his soul is not at rest. So it was with me even in my brightest days. There was uneasiness haunting me because of the knowlege of my past life, the memory of my crime and the fear of detection.

Some people doubt the existence of a personal devil. During these days I came to be almost orthodox on the subject of a personal devil. It seemed that he whispered to me almost audibly, and told me my happiness could not last, that my crime would be found out, that Miss Fawnsworth would learn the story of my past life, that if she, the beautiful, pure Christian that she was, only knew my history and real character, she would fly from me frightened as a dove from a filthy vulture; and thus was I harassed more or less in the midst of the new joy that had come to me.

The year passed. Miss Fawnsworth extended her stay in Shanghai three months longer; three happy months; the memory of them brings to me a rift in the clouds that have settled about me and here in my prison, in the dark nights, lying on my cot, I love to pull down the curtain of my past life up to my meeting with her and, as far as possible, to shut out what has followed those happy months and to think, and dream, and hug to the heart of my memory those golden days.

Before Miss Fawnsworth sailed for the United States we became engaged to be married. I should have come with her, but I was under written contract to remain with my employers for some months later. My salary was now quite large and I knew that I would have great need of this money with which to set up housekeeping after my marriage. Painful as it was, we agreed that she should return home and I should remain some months yet in Shanghai.

When the sad day came I went with her down the river on the little boat, the very craft on which I had first met with her. I shall never forget her graceful form and beautiful face as she leaned on the rail of the ship after I had bidden her farewell on the deck, and looked down at me as I stood on top of our little steamer and she waved her handkerchief as the ship sailed away. I watched her from the top of our boat until the distance swallowed up the ship and it seemed that my heart sank within me.

I occupied myself with my business, found some pleasant pastime with the new acquaintances I had made, practicing the closest economy and looking forward to the happy day when I would sail away to the United States to take my beautiful bride. There were dark hours of trial and temptation and many suggestions that I would be detected if I should ever return to he United States.

The letters came and went on every ship from our American shores. Instead of relaxing, distance only intensified my ardent love and longings for the happiness I felt the future held for me. I gathered from hints in the letters that came to me that Miss Fawnsworth's health was not good. Her brother finally confided to me that her physicians and friends at home were very uneasy about her. My anxiety was almost beyond endurance and I wrote begging her for permission to come to her at once, but she urged me to continue at my post of duty and assured me that she would soon be much better.

Her trouble developed rapidly and the physicians decided that an operation would be necessary. Of course, I knew nothing of this. The day before going upon the table she wrote me a most beautiful letter. It lies here upon my table by me tonight and long before that letter reached me in Shanghai, she was sleeping quietly in her grave and her beautiful spirit had flown away beyond the stars.

I shall not undertake to tell the reader of the disappointment, agony, and desperation that seized my heart with the grip of a demon when the sad news of her death came to me. I felt as if the great Being who knew my secret and my many sins, had intervened and caught the beautiful creature away from the eager arms of a poor wretch that were extended to embrace her. I strove hard for a short time against the waves and billows that went over me, but it was in vain. The change that had come to me for the better was not a change of my moral character so much as a change of my habits, and that upon a selfish basis. It had not been the love of Christ that had so remarkably affected me but the love of a beautiful woman. Had she lived and had our lives been united, it may be that I would have won out in the long run and it may be as the years went by the real beast that lurked in me might have broken loose and brought sorrow to her heart.

I regret to have to confess that I turned to drink to bury my sorrow and soon became unfit for business and lost my position. I recovered somewhat, steadied myself, and determined never again to go back to the awful depths of a gutter drunkard. I was restless and it seemed impossible for me to remain in any one place. I had no desire whatever to come back home, so falling in with a young fellow from Philadelphia, who was going out to India to buy goatskins, I put in what of my little savings I had not squandered and we sailed down to Hongkong, round Singapore, up the Straights and landed in Calcutta.

We traveled extensively in India buying goatskins and shipped them to the United States. The country was so intensely warm that I found I must abstain from strong drink in any considerable quantity or make a quick run to my grave;

and as little promise of happiness as this life held out to me, I dared not take the leap into the uncertainties of the future.

While traveling in India I fell in with a very interesting young missionary engaged in evangelistic work; a young fellow who had come out from my own country some years before and was traveling among the English-speaking churches holding revival meetings. I spent several days in a city where he was engaged in meetings, we stopped at the same hotel, I attended his services and got deeply interested in him and his work. He was a man of culture, of unusual intelligence, and remarkably gifted for the work in which he was engaged. He spoke with great earnestness, sometimes with genuine eloquence and, in the pulpit, in the hotel, and on several long walks which we took together, I was made to feel that I had found in him the highest type of Christian I had ever met. He was fully endued with the spirit of Christ as revealed in the New Testament.

My conscience was somewhat awakened and I was thinking very seriously as I sauntered about the streets and parks and sat in my room waiting for several days to meet a native who represented a large firm engaged in our business, but unfortunately, one day I stepped into a news stand and bought one of the leading magazines from the United States, in which was a lengthy article setting forth the views of a number of leading university presidents and prominent educators who utterly repudiated the old Christian faith, speaking in contemptuous terms of the views of orthodox Christians such as the young man with whom I had been associating. It was like a blighting frost upon the tender plants that were striving to break through the hard ground of my heart into the sunlight of hope and faith, and I flung away every vestige of purpose and, as far as possible, the desire for a better life.

After some time in India, we came on through Aden, up the Red Sea to Port Said. We did some business in goatskins in Egypt and Palestine, came on through Europe, stopped for some time in Paris, where I spent most of my savings and the profits on my recent enterprises, drinking, gambling, seeing the world and plunging into it with a hollow laugh and a hardened heart.

While in Paris I engaged in some enterprises that I had never participated in before in the way of dishonest transactions, trying to reason with myself that this life was all there was for me and I ought to seek to get out of it the most possible. I barely escaped arrest in Paris for my misdemeanors, was shadowed by the police but was able to evade them and slip away for London. Strange to say this new venture in wickedness seemed to affect me as human flesh affects a man-eating tiger which, after having once tasted, he does not relish any other repast than one made up of a human being, and I found arising in me a strange fascination in the secrecy and vigilance necessary to a criminal course. I was possessed with the desire to match my shrewdness against that of the police with the notion that I could commit almost any crime and get away without detection.

I found myself reading with great interest any account of criminal transaction, their escapes, arrests, punishments, etc., and entertained myself and my companions pointing out their mistakes and the clumsiness with which they had managed their affair, and how cleverly it might have been done. This new passion was coming to master me and, strange to say, the appetite of strong drink somewhat abated and while I drank frequently, I was able to so control myself that I rarely felt anything like intoxication.

I spent some months in London, the great rendezvous of thieves, crooks, and criminals of every kind. It was far from my mind to become a sneak thief, or to indulge in any of the worse class crimes, but I had gotten the idea that there was little or no harm in taking fine jewelry or a purse which was left lying around carelessly about a man's premises and indulged in such things with something of the zest with which an old fisherman seeks a clear, rocky stream for bass, or an experienced hunter goes into the mountains for deer.

CHAPTER VIII.

HOMEWARD BOUND.

Finally, there came into me a desire to return to the United States, and, like many another hopeless, hapless human being tossed like driftwood on a stream which is beat first upon this coast and then that, I sailed away for New York. Upon landing I undertook to get a letter to my father and learned in a note from the postmaster that he had died quite a while ago and that my mother, whose health was poor, was spending the winter either in southern Florida or in Havana, Cuba. This information was something of a relief to me. I felt sure that if there was any better world father and John had met there in great peace, and faulty as I was, I felt it would be my duty to visit my mother if I knew where to find her, but so long as I did not know where she was, I was under no obligation to visit her and therefore tossed away all thought of any sort of responsibility and plunged into the seething human ocean of sin in the great American metropolis.

In time I drifted to Chicago where I was arrested for burglary and brought to trial, but escaped the justice which I deserved for lack of testimony; drifted to St. Louis, helped to rob a bank in a little western town, got away with a few thousand to my share which was soon squandered, and roamed about the west assuming to be an easy-going, careless fellow seeking the boldest and most wicked of associates, never missing an opportunity to talk against religion and the Bible and reading with interest and, as near delight as was possible for myself to feel, anything, and everything that was said in the *Outlook, Literary Digest,* daily papers, and other literature against the old faith of the devout people who really loved God and trusted in Jesus for salvation. Those men who boast of being higher critics and who cast doubt on the inspiration of the Scriptures, and the awful responsibilities which a man must meet in the other world for his wicked conduct here, may be sure that their writings are hailed with delight in bar-rooms, brothels, and all dives of sin and iniquity. Men who give themselves up to wickedness nevertheless are men. They have some intelligence, they have some conscience however dead it may be and, again and again, there is an inclination to be stirred with fear lest they must meet, and be held responsible for their conduct at some judgment bar or in some awful afterworld where the heart and life are uncovered in the white light to the gaze of the intelligent universe.

To destroy these convictions among the vicious class, is to take a very dangerous risk and I predict that the time is coming in this Union when there will spring up from the seeds of doubt that are now being sown, a fearful condition of utter

unbelief and widespread anarchy. It is not at all
impossible that in this unbelief in the colleges
and universities of the country, lie the germs that
will lead on to a state of society that will ulti-
mately result in the overthrow of the republic.

The great civilizations of ancient times were
destroyed. The great cities, centers of commerce,
art and culture are now places of desolation and
waste. History makes plain to us the fact that
this desolation and waste were brought about by
the abounding wickedness of the people.

My experience forces me to believe that as the
Bible has been held up to ridicule, and disbelief
in the fundamentals of the gospel has been taught
far and near, and faith has dwindled and died,
along with the increase of doubt, there has come
an increase of deviltry and disregard of great
laws and forces that lie at the very foundation of
civilization.

The man with strong, natural inclinations to
sin, and strong outward temptation urging him
on in the direction of his natural inclination, with
the fear of consequences removed, is a very dangerous factor in society. I understand very readily that there is a class of people who will ridicule such preaching as this from the cell of a
prison; there are others, who, remembering that
I was well born, and grew up in a Christian home
with all the advantages of good society and college and university life, will realize that after

such varied experiences as I have passed through that I have a right to speak. That it is my duty to do so; that it is perfectly consistent that I should point out with the finger of warning to the young men of the rising generation the pathway that led to my undoing. There is no doubt in my mind, but today, I might be a happy and useful member of society had I retained the faith and followed the example of my devout father instead of listening to the sophistries and ridicule of conceited college professors, who were as unsound in their philosophy as they perhaps were, in some instances, in moral character.

In my drifting westward, I was finally brought up on the Pacific coast and landed in San Francisco, the center of worldliness, with the same reckless "don't care," with reference to the hereafter. The rebuilding of that city had drawn to the place great numbers of strong, rough, determined men and it was the general belief that whether God had used the earthquake for the destruction of the old city or not, that the new city had as far surpassed the old one in wickedness, as it did in the magnificence of its modern architecture.

The very atmosphere of San Francisco seems surcharged with movement and energy. The ordinary man farther East, seems to become extraordinary in whatever line he follows, when he strikes the rushing current of life in San Francisco, and

I here turned myself loose in wickedness with the notion that it would be quite easy to evade the representatives of the law. I was soon however apprehended and brought before the courts, was found guilty and served my first term in prison. Six months penned up behind iron bars seemed only to whet my appetite for adventure along the line of my profession and, on being set free, I started East with a couple of acquaintances who, like myself, had wandered out West, and being unwilling to return to New York without the means for high living, we determined to rob a train. This was the most dangerous and desperate enterprise in all my history as a criminal.

We selected our place near the top of a long grade in the mountains of Nevada, carefully planned the enterprise, but unwisely spent a few days in a village near the place where we proposed the robbery, which we carried out quite successfully, so far as the mere transaction was concerned, but not so far as the amount of booty obtained, which was trifling in comparison with what we had promised ourselves. As soon as the robbery became known, the officials of the village on missing us suspected that we were the guilty parties, struck our trail and pressed us hard for several days.

One of my companions was shot to death. Poor fellow! To all human appearances he went out utterly unprepared. We had abandoned our horses and had gone on foot into the mountain crags where we were closely pressed by a posse of officers who never missed an opportunity to take a snipe at us with their long-range rifles. One of my associates and myself ran some twenty paces from a huge boulder to a cliff where we could not only screen ourselves for the time, but from behind which we could travel quite a distance without exposing ourselves to the fire of our pursuers. When number three undertook to run across the clear space he was fired upon and hit in two places. One shot broke his left limb below the knee and the other, passing through his body, perforated one of his lungs and cut a vein from which the poor fellow soon bled to death. When we saw that he had fallen we waited for him, and he dragged himself to the protection of the cliff where we pulled off his coat, made a pillow for his head and, while my associate climbed to the top of the rock and took several shots at our pursuers which forced them to halt and conceal themselves, I gave our dying friend some water out of a canteen which I carried and asked him if I could render him any service. He gave me his watch and what valuables he had on his person and looking me in the face said to me: "I have never told you my true name; I came of good family and enjoyed excellent advantages but wasted them. Many a time during my reckless life I have determined to down-brakes and change for the better, but it is all up with me now. It seems hard to die in this place alone, but it looks like one who was getting as little real happiness out of life as I was ought not to complain." He weakened rapidly from the loss of blood, became quite exhausted and fainted but rallied somewhat; his mind wandered, he called for his mother, then seemed to be greatly frightened at something, struggled almost to a sitting posture and fell back, stone dead.

I called to my companion who was firing away at the top of the rock, that he was dead and we had better continue our flight. He leaped down and we ran away, but were soon hemmed in by some parties who had made a circuit during the delay, and forced us to change our course. We separated and I ran on not knowing whither I went or what had become of my comrade. I afterward learned that he was captured a short time after our separation.

The sun was burning hot on the barren mountain, the glare almost blinded me and perspiration trickled down my face into my eyes. I had eaten all of my scanty rations and was weak and hungry and the water in my canteen was hot, though I treasured it to its last precious drops which I drank and threw away the canteen.

A feeling of desolation came over me. Here I was, a desolate, ruined, hunted man. In the nature of things, every good citizen on earth must be against me and was bound to unite with the

forces that pursued me as a wretch unfit for free-
dom and a dangerous menace to society. As I
stumbled on, I determined if I could make my es-
cape this time, I would reform my life and strive
once more for better things. Sometimes I had a
strong impulse to turn and stand at bay and
fighting to the last to court death. But bad as I
was, I couldn't find it in my heart to shoot down
another one of my fellowmen, and I was somewhat opposed to being shot. I could hear the yells
and shots of my pursuers. There were not less
than fifteen or twenty men following me in the
shape of a crescent on the right hand and on the
left, I judged very close and now and then I
caught the glimpse of a man dodging from rock to
rock about even with me.

I had climbed up out of a depression to a slope
reaching the edge of a broad plain comparatively
free from any obstruction or place of conceal-
ment. It was my judgment if I undertook to
cross this plain, I would be shot down, so I un-
buckled my cartridge belt and flung it away,
tossed my pistols and rifle into a gulch, pulled off
my coat, made a pillow of it and lay down utterly
exhausted in the shadow of a great boulder. As I
lay there waiting for my captors, not knowing but
they would perforate me with bullets the moment
they saw me and caring little what happened, my
life passed before me. I thought of my home, of
those who had once loved me with tender solici-

tude, of the happy days I had known in my early life, of the battles and defeats that had come to me later on and I was forced to admit that whatever the opinion of the higher critics and college professors with reference to the inspiration of the Scriptures, there was one statement written in the Old Book that my own experience had sadly verified, namely: "The way of the transgressor is hard."

CHAPTER IX.

TAKEN PRISONER.

As I lay there waiting and thinking, I thrust my hand into the pocket of the left breast of my shirt, and took out a small photograph and a little rosebud wrapped in a piece of oiled paper. The photograph was of the woman of whom I have written, whom I have loved so dearly and who was torn so soon from me by death. The rosebud was the one she had given me on the deck of the little steamer the first day I had looked into her angel face. As I looked at these little tokens, my heart cried out within me against the cruel fate which had followed me, and for the first time in many days tears came into my eyes. Folding up the precious little mementos I replaced them where I had carried them for so long and, overcome with fasting and fatigue, I fell asleep.

After some time, I know not how long, I was aroused by a voice saying, "Wake up here!" and opening my eyes I found I was surrounded by a group of not less than half a dozen men with their Winchester rifles pointed at me. "Throw up your hands!" My hands went up as I rose to a sitting posture and I said: "Gentlemen, I am your prisoner. I have thrown away my arms and shall make no resistance." One of the men came forward and with a good deal of display of authority clicked handcuffs upon my wrists and jerked me to a standing posture.

Fortunately for me there had been no one killed in the train robbery, or I believe these men would have made short work with me. As it was there was much profanity, rough talk, and threats, but having killed one of our number, and captured the other two of us, they were very well pleased with themselves and, after the first excitement which followed getting me safely into their clutches, they treated me as kindly as I could expect under the circumstances.

We had a rough journey back from the mountains and attracted great attention at every point where we stopped for refreshments, took a train, or changed cars. I was finally landed safely behind the iron bars of a prison, and I must confess a sense of relief came over me after the excitement of the robbery, the flight into the mountains, the chase and exhaustion, and then the weary journey of return. I seemed to be dead inside, feeling was almost entirely gone from me and I was more brute than human. I ate my food, slept soundly, read the newspapers, looked back over the past, which seemed like a troubled dream, and into the future, which looked blank and dark enough. I had sown the seeds of sin and was reaping the harvest of sorrow. As the days went by my nerves relaxed, my whole physical and nervous constitution rested from the tremendous tension of the past few years, and I seemed to wake out of a strange dream. Like the Prodigal Son of whom I had read in the good old Book in my boyhood days, I came to myself, and realized that I was indeed in a far country. But it seemed too late to resolve to arise and go to my father's house. Strong iron bars stood between me and the home of my childhood. My father was dead and gone; my mother, I had no idea where she was, and was fully determined that if it were possible for me to keep my secret, she should know nothing of my checkered career.

There are many such men in the world. Men who have drifted from their homes and then fallen into sin and crime. They are lost to all who ever knew them, lost to society, to hope, liberty, and they wear out their poor miserable lives toiling in some prison, concealing their identity while their sad hearts quietly eat themselves away in bitterness and disappointment.

The reader must not understand that I was a penitent. I had not reached the point where I grieved for my sins; I grieved that I had been detected in my sins and brought to account for them.

As the time of my trial approached, which was very soon after my incarceration, I felt no disposition to employ a lawyer, I never had denied my crime, I felt sure of punishment and doggedly awaited it, feeling that it would be something of a relief to begin to work out the weary years be-

tween me and liberty, with some sort of employment that would give exercise to my body and a
degree of activity to my mind.

My trial was quite a formal affair and I was
sent to the penitentiary in short order for a pe-
riod of not less than ten, and not more than fifteen years.

When I was brought to the prison and stood
inside of a circle line, and my clothes taken from
me and burned, my hair shorn close to my head,
and I was bathed and put into a striped suit, my
heart sank within me and there settled upon me a
dead heavy weight of disappointment, shame, and
protest against my fate which seemed to blind my
soul, and crush my very body.

I was one of the practical evil results of modern popular unbelief, which is disseminated from
so many colleges and universities, and not a few
pulpits, and that too by men who are so shallow
and ignorant of the real philosophy of life that
they imagine themselves to be benefactors of society.

It was my good fortune to be placed in a prison
whose chief warden was perhaps as suitable a man
for the position he occupies as any other man in
the country. He was genuinely interested in the
welfare of his prisoners, he was careful to see that
we had a sufficiency of healthy food, proper baths,
and were made as comfortable in our cells as prisoners could hope to be even in these progressive

times, when the spirit of humanitarianism is
abroad in the land.

Our chaplain, at the time of my incarceration,
was merely a political chaplain. He had been appointed because of the pull he had with certain
men in office, and not because of any special
qualifications he had to fill the office; he was of no
special benefit either to the prisoners or the state.
There did not seem to be anything especially bad
in him; he was simply a figure-head. He went
through the discharge of his duties in a perfunc-
tory way, drew his salary, came to the prison when
he had to, and got away as soon as possible.

Many of the guards, and not a few of the foremen about the prison were coarse, rough men who
seemed to take pleasure in the discomfort of the
unfortunate men under their control. I am quite
safe in saying that there is no doubt but many of
our penal institutions, instead of being places of
penitence and reform, are schools of vice in which
men are hardened in sin and crime. Several of
the foremen and guards of our institution seem to
take delight in annoying and torturing those
under their control, and not a few of our prisoners
were so hardened and imbruted in their crimes,
that they in turn sought every opportunity to pro-
voke and in any possible way annoy those who
had charge of them. Of course, they sought to do
this so as not to bring the wrath of their tormen-
tors down upon themselves.

On entering the prison I resolved to be as good
a prisoner as possible and make the best of a bad
situation. To be sure, I was overwhelmed with
my situation, discouraged, and outraged, and
somewhat sullen. I was put to work in a paint
shop. My employment was that of staining and
varnishing chairs. I soon learned to execute my
work with a degree of efficiency and was able to
complete my task and have some time to work for
myself, which I did with some financial advantage,
saving up a little money which I deposited with
one of our prison officials, taking a receipt for
same. The money was to be turned over to me
when my time was up, or at any time I should
demand it.

After my first year in prison we were fortunate
in securing in the chaplain a man who really loved
the poor souls of the unfortunate fellows he had
come to minister to. He spent almost all of his
time in the prison, moving around among the
prisoners, speaking kind words, looking after our
sick, finding out about the location of the families
and affairs of our poor boys, and writing letters
for those who could not write for themselves. His
influence for good was felt in the prison in a very
short time after his arrival. He preached with
great earnestness, not infrequently weeping while
offering salvation to the poor condemned wretches
who sat before him. His influence affected the
guards, there was less of roughness among them,

there was general improvement in the discipline and conduct of the prisoners, and not long after the arrival of our new chaplain, several of our men claimed to be converted, and the change in their lives and conduct gave good reason to believe that their claim was not without foundation.

Among the religious workers who came to the prison there was a man and woman who played the organ and sang. They had a beautiful little girl, a flaxen-haired child, about three or four years of age of whom the prisoners were very fond. Up to this time I had taken no part in religious services. My seat in the chapel was far back from the front and while it was my purpose to treat the whole matter of religion and personal responsibility with indifference, in spite of myself. I soon found some sort of an awakening going on within me. I got interested in the chaplain, the young man and his wife and baby. I found a longing within my heart to get the beautiful little girl in my arms, and one afternoon as the gentleman and his wife came out of the chapel I reached out my hands to the little creature and she came to me very gladly, patting my cheek and said in her baby way, "Mr. Man, where is your little dirl?" and looked into my face with such tender and kindly interest that my heart began to throb, and there came rushing into my mind a thought of the silent grave away up in one of the middle states where slept the beautiful woman who had loved me so dearly and promised to bless me so much.

This little child awakened in me a genuine interest, and I found myself longing for the time when she would come with her parents to the prison. Her presence in the chapel gave the entire service a new meaning to me and scarcely a Sabbath afternoon passed that we did not have some sort of friendly chat, and frequently it was my privilege to carry the little creature in my arms to the gate leading from the prison. I found myself preserving any little card, clipping, some picture from a magazine, or whittling out at odd moments a little toy, to please the fancy of this little friend of mine. Her parents seemed pleased with the kindly feeling that had sprung up between the little girl and myself, and while it did not occur to me at the time, I am quite sure now that they were earnestly praying that this beautiful little creature might in some way thaw out my heart and sullen nature, and open up for me the return road to a better life.

CHAPTER X.

A SYMPATHETIC FRIEND.

At the close of my last chapter I was telling the readers of the new interest in life which had sprung up within me, because of the acquaintance and friendship I had formed for the little daughter, whose parents came for religious service on the Sabbath afternoons in our prison chapel. This friendship deepened into a genuine love on my part and, strange as it may seem, I had every reason to believe the little child had a genuine love for me. She reminded me very much of the beautiful creature who had given me the rosebud on the steamboat of which I had spoken before, and somehow the hardness in me melted under her influence and almost unconsciously, I found myself having a more kindly feeling toward everybody and in me there were rising up hopes that even yet there might be for me some victory and usefulness in the world.

Meanwhile I had joined a Sabbath school class, and had for my teacher a quiet, little widow, who was well advanced in years and certainly one of the most kind-hearted and earnest Christian women I have ever met. She seemed to be full of faith and love for everybody. I learned afterward that her father, though a member of a very respectable family, when she was a little girl, had been sentenced to prison because of an unfortunate appropriation of funds which had been intrusted to him. He had died in prison and this tender-hearted woman who had loved and stood by him faithfully through the years of his disgrace and suffering, had formed a great, deep Christian love and solicitude for all the men who wore stripes in the prison in which her father had been incarcerated, and from which he had been taken forth and buried in a grave of shame.

She soon found out that I was a skeptic and labored faithfully to rid me of my doubts and lead me to faith in the Christ. My faith faculty seemed to be almost paralyzed or destroyed. Her solicitude was so great, her motives evidently so unselfish that I could not account for her attitude toward me in any other way than that she possessed a love and sympathy for us poor prisoners that did not belong naturally to human nature. I figured that it must be something that had come into her heart through acquaintance with the Man of Galilee.

I remember one day she brought me a little book, the title of which I cannot exactly remember. It had been written by a Catholic priest, and was an answer to some lecture or article from the celebrated infidel, Robert Ingersoll. It was the most scathing piece of sarcasm I ever saw in print. The priest had handled the skeptic without gloves. He had punctured the windbags of his opposer, laid bare the falsehoods contained in his statements, and held him up to public ridicule in a most remarkable way. One could not read the book without being profoundly impressed with the remarkable skill of the priest.

Ingersoll had been something of a champion of mine before, but time and again while reading this book I was forced to laugh heartily at my hero. The priest certainly placed him in a very unenviable light and swept away many of the false notions under which I had been taking refuge. I remember one paragraph in the book read almost like the following:

"Mr. Ingersoll's friends, to prove that he was a man of infinite jest, liked to tell of his war record, which consisted in marching down south and marching home again. Mr. Ingersoll was captured by some southern soldiers in a hog pen, and Gen. Forrest, whose sarcasm was as keen as his sword, exchanged him for a mule, and Col. Ingersoll hastened back to the north where he found more money, and less danger in ridiculing the Bible, than in meeting a brave rebel soldier with a gun in his hand. If Gen. Grant, and the boys in blue who followed him to war, had have had as little fear of God, and as much fear of rebel soldiers as Col. Ingersoll had, there would now be six million slaves in the United States."

This put me to thinking about the leading infidels in whom I had been interested, and whom I had believed were such great men, and I asked myself what good these men had done with their teachings, which had destroyed the faith of multitudes of people. Who had been made better, or more hopeful and happy by giving up his faith in Jesus Christ, the immortality of the soul, and a happy hereafter? Who in the wide world could say that he was a better and happier man because of the writings of Hume, Voltaire, Tom Paine, or Robert Ingersoll?

As I lay awake at night on my little bed these thoughts rambled through my mind for many hours. I asked myself what skeptic, from the college professor who had first shaken my faith in the Bible, and genuineness of the Christian religion, down to the poorest, most degraded sot I had ever heard swearing over a glass of whiskey in a bar-room, who of all these doubters had brought any help or strength or light into my life. Not one of them and as I thought over the matter I was forced to believe that not one of these men was himself a happy man.

Come to think of it, happiness rises more out of our hopes for the future, than out of our enjoyment of things past or present, and the Christian always has a hopeful future. When everything else fails, he can take Job's view of the situation and rejoice because of what he expects in time to come. He carries in his heart the hope of a resurrection and a life with his Lord on the other side which shall be free from all temptation, disease, sorrowful separation, or sin, and this hope is an anchorage to him in all of the vicissitudes of life.

I thought over the people who had been of any value to me, who had wakened anything good in me, and without an exception they were Christians. There was my devout old father, faithful and patient and true now no doubt in heaven; and there was my brother John; all the while, in the days of my unbelief and sin, I could see John as a white saint, no stains on him, no selfishness in him, no blot of unbelief, and I never could feel as if John were dead. Somehow in the midst of my infidelity I had a profound feeling that John was living conscious and happy, somewhere. Then there was the sweet angel of the rosebud. How firm was her faith! How spotless her life! How radiant her hope! It could not be that she had been blotted out of existence. No, No! Somewhere in God's universe she and John were together and if, in the other world, people remember, and if they love those whom they loved on earth, doubtless they feel for them genuine solicitude, and if they are with the compassionate Christ who never turned away a penitent heart on earth, they were evidently praying for me.

I shuddered at the thought that they should know anything of the life I had been living, and my present humiliation and disgrace and yet there was within me a hope that they did know and that they did pray for me. And thus the weeks passed by, my mind and thought throughout the busy day at the table, in my cell at night, turning again and again to this subject.

My Sunday school teacher had brought me a Bible with many texts marked in red and blue pencil, and I was reading this with an interest I had never known before. Many times it seemed to me as if the type almost spoke with a tongue. It thrilled and startled me. Nothing struck me more than the words in John's gospel: "For God so loved the world, that he gave his only begotten Son, that whosoever believeth in him shall not perish, but have everlasting life." This fastened my attention. Could it be possible that God loved me? Then why this checkered life of mine, and this miserable failure? But I reasoned that notwithstanding God's love I was a free agent, it had been my own choice, the things in my history and life which had brought sorrow and shame had come because of disobedience to God's commands, and sins against his righteous laws. The ruin which had come to me was no proof that God did not love me. The scriptures themselves had plainly said "Whatsoever a man soweth, that shall he also reap," and I had sown with a liberal hand, and now my harvest time had come and with blistered, weary hands I struggled in a vast harvest field that swept far beyond the horizon, and promised me nothing but failure and disappointment and shame, not only in this life, but also in the life which was to come, if the old book was true, and if the only people that I had ever known who were really happy, and who had been of any value to me, were not fearfully deluded in their faith and hopes. In the midst of all these thoughts passing again and again through my mind, there rose very clearly the memory of my own conversion. It stood out with a freshness and reality which I had not known for years. Without doubt in that old Methodist Church one night at the altar I had really met with Jesus. He had blotted out my sins, lifted up my burdens, and brought a strange restful peacefulness into my heart. The days following this remarkable experience were some of the happiest days I had ever known. There could be no doubt about it.

I had been metamorphosed at the college, my professors had led me on step by step into the dark regions of unbelief, they had robbed me of my childhood faith, and then leaving me bruised and wounded they had passed on the other side. Now, in my misfortune, no infidel came to me with a prattling babe to take into my arms, or beautiful flower to cheer me for a little while, a good book with which to wear away the time, or kindly word of encouragement and promise of forgiveness of my sins and happiness and rest in the days to come. This, the Christians had done, the followers of Jesus were eager to help me and never scemed so happy as when I gave any sort of evidence of repentance, or of turning for salvation and hope to the Savior of whom they spoke so much and with such confident assurance.

I was now devoting almost all my spare time to the reading of good books. I lost all taste for skeptical works or trashy novels, and found myself interested in religious literature—tracts, religious papers, the biographies of Christians, missionaries, ministers. How absolutely different they were from myself, and the people with whom I had associated. No doubt they had their weaknesses, made their mistakes, and had their sorrows, but in spite of all this they lived in an entirely different world from that in which I had my miserable existence.

My little Sunday school teacher was radiant with happiness over the change that had come to me, and urged me to give my heart to Jesus, and I found myself wishing that I could do this thing which seemed so impossible; and in the sighs and groans which came involuntarily from my lips, there were words of prayer, and I was surprised and startled to hear myself saying: "Have mercy on me, help me, forgive me." The reader may be sure that I was very far from happiness. I had no hopes or rest, day or night, but there was this change that had come to me, I scarcely knew how or when, my profanity was all gone, my skepticism had about withered, I had no sort of pleasure any more in any sort of rough talk or ridicule of religion and there came to me a flash of hopefulness and at last a dream of the possibility of pardon and peace somewhere in the future.

CHAPTER XI.

A PARDONED SINNER.

There were quite a number of unbelievers among
the prisoners shut up with me, and while we had
but little communication with each other, our new
chaplain, the earnest man of whom I have spoken,
visited and talked with us and got at our hearts'
secrets. This led him to preach a sermon against
skepticism, not perhaps exactly that, but a sermon
in which he laid down the grounds upon which
the Christian could find a reasonable basis for
his faith. I remember one morning he spoke especially of what he called the "Prophetic Method."
He pointed out the fact that God had so arranged
the plan of revelation that the honest man who
gave the subject proper investigation could hardly
evade believing. He showed how the prophets had
foretold many centuries before, the things that
did afterward come to pass, and he showed how
these prophets were so many and minute that
guesswork was out of the question. He proved
that these prophecies were contained in old rec-
ords that had stood the test of criticism, that
critics and infidels themselves were bound to admit that the Old Testament Scriptures had existed
long before the birth of Christ, and that in Christ's
life, ministry, and crucifixion these prophecies had
been fulfilled in such exact detail, and that too in
many instances by men who knew nothing of the

prophecies and had no faith in Christ, that no honest man could conclude that these men had any purpose to fulfill the prophecies or any knowledge, or remote thought that they were doing so. For example; he referred to the prophecy of Christ being crucified between two thieves and being buried in a rich man's grave. He also called attention to the fact that the prophet had said that "none of his bones should be broken" and quite a number of prophecies which I cannot recall just now, but made a very decided impression upon me at the time and were so very clear that it seems to me impossible to answer them.

My candid judgment is that the average infidel has not made anything like a careful and honest investigation of the evidences of Christianity and the many proofs in favor of the inspiration of the Scriptures. In many instances the skeptic is not seeking for proofs of the existence of God and the inspiration of the Bible. Generally the skeptic is a wicked man and like I had done for many years, he is so anxious to avoid the consequences of his sins that he would be only too glad if he could become fully convinced that there is no God and that the Scriptures are not inspired.

I became so interested in the subject that I was led to ask the chaplain several questions which resulted in his securing for me a number of books which I read with great interest. Among them was a large old volume called "The Elements of

Divinity." He marked several chapters and paragraphs for me to read which very clearly settled all my questions, removed my doubts and left me fully persuaded that the Bible is an inspired book and that Jesus Christ is able to save all men, even the most unworthy, from all sin. This matter fully settled, the memory of my conversion as a boy loomed up before me in the clearest light imaginable, and along with it came trooping about me a harrowing memory of my many sins. There was one scripture that pierced me through as a sharp sword; that passage which says: "No murderer shall enter into the kingdom of heaven." This seemed to shut the door effectually in my face. I called our chaplain's attention to it one day and asked him if it would be interpreted to mean that the poor fellow in prison who had committed murder had no hope for salvation. He explained that a man who was a murderer at heart, whether he had killed his man or not, could not enter into the kingdom of heaven, that the scripture referred more to a murderous condition of heart than to any act a man might have committed, and that it was possible for even a murderer to so repent of his wicked deed and trust in Jesus that all malice and hatred would be removed from the heart, and also the stain of sin placed there by any murderous act, desire or intention of the past.

He convinced me that this scripture did not

close the door of hope to my disturbed soul. I
spent much time in prayer. Sometimes much of
the night passed with me upon my knees at the
side of my cot calling for mercy. My fountain of
tears was well-nigh dried up. I often wished that
I could weep but I had become so hardened by infidelity and sin that it seemed almost impossible
for me to weep. The chaplain, and my Sabbath
school teacher took a great interest in me and one
Sabbath afternoon when they had called for those
who desired salvation to remain in the chapel after the service were dismissed, several of the prisoners, myself among them, remained for prayer
and instruction. We were called forward to kneel
at a bench which was put out near the preacher's
stand and while the choir sang and the Christian
friends instructed us we waited in prayer.

I shall not undertake to tell the reader of the
startling and awful sins which passed before me
that afternoon. They stood out with huge deform-
ity and blackness. The time I had wasted in
school, my neglected opportunities, my disregard
of the instructions and entreaties of my father,
the waste and folly at gambling and drink, the profanity, dishonesty, and untruthfulness of my past,
all crowded about me like so many devils and
seemed to hiss and jeer and ridicule in my ears
till it seemed the blood would almost congeal in
my veins. The cold perspiration broke out on my
body and my hands seemed to be as cold as if

chilled with death. I fell into a state of blank despair. It seemed that I could neither weep nor
pray nor trust. But the friends urged me, sang
and prayed and insisted that I should utter certain
prayers regardless of my doubts and feelings of
despair. These exercises seemed to give me some
relief for a time, but my hopes and better feelings
were very temporary and there came to me a fearful conviction that I had sinned away my day of
grace. I had not only violated God's divine law,
but I had rejected his compassionate mercy, I had
broken his commandments, and sneered at the
Christ who had come to save me. I had denied
his very existence, I had uttered most fearful and
profane things with reference to his religion, his
character and his death. Was it possible that he
could forgive one like myself? I seemed to give
up all hope and concluded that my eternal punishment was a fixed and awful fact, but there came
into my mind a positive resolution to sin no more,
and even if I should at last be shut up in the re-
gion of lost spirits, I determined to defend God,
to say that my punishment was just, that there
was no one to blame for my sad end except myself.
If I should be lost, I determined to become a wit-
ness to the goodness and mercy and justice of God
even in the midst of the profane and miserable
souls in the depths of outer darkness. Despairing
as I was, dead as seemed all hope to me, urged
by my friends I continued to pray. All at once my

burden vanished. Fear seemed to depart absolutely from my heart, I rose at once in triumphant
laughter and praise and got the chaplain into my
striped arms and held him to my heart. It seemed
to me that I loved everybody in all the wide world.

Some of the guards and the prisoners came back
into the chapel and as I finally passed out, they
cast some taunting words at me, giving me to understand that there was no better scheme to undertake to secure a pardon or parole than that I
should make much of religious matters. But I was
so wonderfully blessed and for some days so graciously kept, that I felt comparatively indifferent
to the taunts of the guards and prisoners.

The change that had come to me was marvelous
beyond all of my power to describe. My cell seemed to be a little palace and I remembered in joy
that I had heard my old father sing a song in
which were these words: "Prisons would palaces
prove if Jesus would dwell with me there."

How real all things became to me. How clear,
true and reasonable the Scriptures, how wicked
and unreasonable it was to sin; profanity and all
harsh and vulgar words became offensive, the finer
sensibilities awakened in my nature. Old things
had passed away and I was certainly in Christ a
new creature. I felt no shame or hesitancy in telling every one that I was a Christian, that I had
found in Jesus a Savior. The delight of our chaplain and my Sunday school teacher seemed to have

no bounds. They rejoiced with me, so did all of the Christian prisoners, and not a few of those who were not converted seemed to be profoundly interested and genuinely pleased that I had found forgiveness.

I read the Scriptures with great delight and it was sweet to go into my little cell and betake myself to my knees. I availed myself of every opportunity to speak a kind word of exhortation to prisoners, guard, or visitors, and feel confident that my labors were not in vain in the Lord for not long after my conversion there were several others brought very consciously and very blessedly into a gracious relation with Christ, I think I may safely say as the fruit of my personal work.

I confessed my real name to the warden of the penitentiary and with the assistance of my chaplain wrote quite a number of letters to parties whom I had treated grossly, confessed my sin to them, begged their forgiveness, and told them that Christ had graciously saved me by his grace.

Having been skeptical, I now found real delight in reading the very best books I could get hold of whose authors were making war on unbelief of every kind. I enjoyed a little book called "The Man of Galilee" which was written by a Bishop Haygood, I think, of Georgia. It was a wonderful little volume.

I sought every opportunity to put books and tracts into the hands of prisoners whom I had found skeptical. I fully realize that I am suffering the just reward of my deeds and should not blame other people. At the same time it is perfectly clear to me that if I had gotten into some good, religious school, instead of the skeptical institution where I was robbed of my faith, I would no doubt have been a happy and useful citizen instead of having lived a miserably wicked life and being shut up here in prison through these weary years with but little probability of much usefulness in the time to come. If the words of a prisoner are worth anything, I would most earnestly urge parents and guardians to keep children under their care out of skeptical colleges. They will find it almost impossible to stem the tide of ridicule and unbelief that is so common among college professors and students, and so likely to spring up in the conditions surrounding the average institution of learning.

CHAPTER XII.

THE RAINBOW OF PROMISE.

I feel that my story is told and my confession made, and it is hardly worth while for me to hold my readers longer. I am the legitimate fruit, the sad outcome of two conditions that exist widespread in our country today. Conditions as unfortunate as could well be imagined. One, a lax family government, a lack of authority to command, discipline, control, and give the authority to the home, in the building of character among the children that can stand the test. Nothing can take the place of home discipline, nothing can atone for the wickedness and waste of manhood and womanhood that will manifest itself in life when a generation has grown up, without proper family government. There are many very good people, moral and religious, earnest and truthful, who are negligent and lax at this point. If my father could have had control over me and taught me strict, implicit obedience, I am confident I should never have seen the inside of these walls.

My mother was an intelligent, good woman, but she had no proper appreciation of the importance of careful and rigid discipline over a boy. It is too late, however, to lament these things with reference to myself, but I should certainly feel glad if some one might be benefited by what I have had to say here. The home must have order, there must be some sort of rule and regulation, and day and night the children, without hesitation or fretfulness, must be brought to obey their parents, or they will bring grief to them in the end.

The other condition to which I refer, of which I am a victim, are the loose teachings in our schools. The infidelity and unbelief in the Scriptures, in God, in Christ, in the Holy Ghost, in the future punishment of the wicked, in the supernatural power of regeneration and sanctification, in great essentials of revealed religion, and genuine experience. I am amazed at the startling amount of infidelity that is blasting the rising generation, that is taking the foundations from under the young manhood and womanhood who are receiving college and university educations. I am surprised that the religious press of the country does not cry out in constant and vigorous protest, and that the pulpits of the country do not fight against this rising and sweeping tide of unbelief. I suppose, that the lethargy and seeming indifference arises out of the fact that many editors, and prominent preachers are themselves, without a strong and active faith in Christ, and a deep and warm love for the truth. Their faith is defective, their zeal is cool, they are seeking degrees, office, and larger salaries, no doubt many of them are not willing to take any risk of arousing against themselves criticism or opposition. They choose rather to let the faith go than earnestly contend, and take the awful risk of a generation of people who spurn the Bible, and turn their backs on the great doctrine of the Messiahship of Jesus Christ.

I have had golden opportunities in the world; the lack of home discipline and skeptical teachings in the colleges, made me unfit for an honorable place in life, increasing my wickedness and irreverence which made of me a criminal, and has shut me up in prison, and but for the devout love and zeal of a few of Christ's little ones, who would cheerfully die for the truth, who sought me out and led me to repentance and faith, I should in the end have been shut up in hell.

I look forward to the future not without hope. Not only is he, our great deliverer, able to save us from all sin, but he is wonderfully powerful to deliver us from evil consequence, and in spite of our failures, to bring to us happiness and victory. If my health should be preserved, and I should live to wear out my sentence, or if the clemency of those in authority should see fit to trust me again, a free man in society, I shall earnestly seek to redeem the past somewhat with a devoted, upright, and earnest life. I can conceive of nothing that would bring to me such great pleasure, as would be mine, could I in some way influence the students of our colleges and universities, who are traveling in the path that led me so far from the right way, to give up their unbelief and turn to inspired truth for guidance and salvation.

With malice toward none and charity for all, I remain, faithfully and gratefully yours.

THE END.